Just in Rhyme

IN
BLOOM

by Toni McKay-Lawton

Illustrated by Eddie Manning

Ransom

bluebells gather in the dell
and nestle in a glade
a leafy canopy is best
as bluebells love the shade

daisies are delightful flowers
with petals white and shining
they sit together in the grass
their yellow faces smiling

the snowdrops are a tiny bunch
who come out when it's chilly
they sit together under trees
all pretty, white and frilly

primroses sit in little clumps
in moss they're warm and cosy
they come up in the spring time
and look lovely in a posy

the dandelion dances
in amongst the grass
his fluffy yellow face
is glowing as you pass